exclamation mark

by amy krouse rosenthal & tom lichtenheld

SCHOLASTIC PRESS • NEW YORK

! He stood out from the very beginning.

He stood out here.

He stood out there.

It seemed like the only time he didn't stand out

was when he was asleep.

He tried everything to be more like them.

But he just wasn't like everyone else.

Period.

He was confused,  flummoxed,

and deflated.

He even thought about running away.

Then, one day . . .

What grade are you in?
What's your favorite color?

Do you like frogs?
What's your favorite ice cream?
When's your birthday?
Know any good jokes?
Do you wanna race to the corner?
Is there an echo in here?
Is there an echo in here?
What's your favorite movie?
Do you know what makes gravity?
Why do you look so surprised?
Am I boring you?
Do you think a snail could go around the world?
So, what do you want to do?
Who's taller, you or me?
What do you want to be when you grow up?

He didn't know he had it in him.

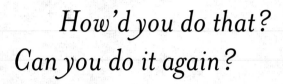

He wasn't sure, so he started small.

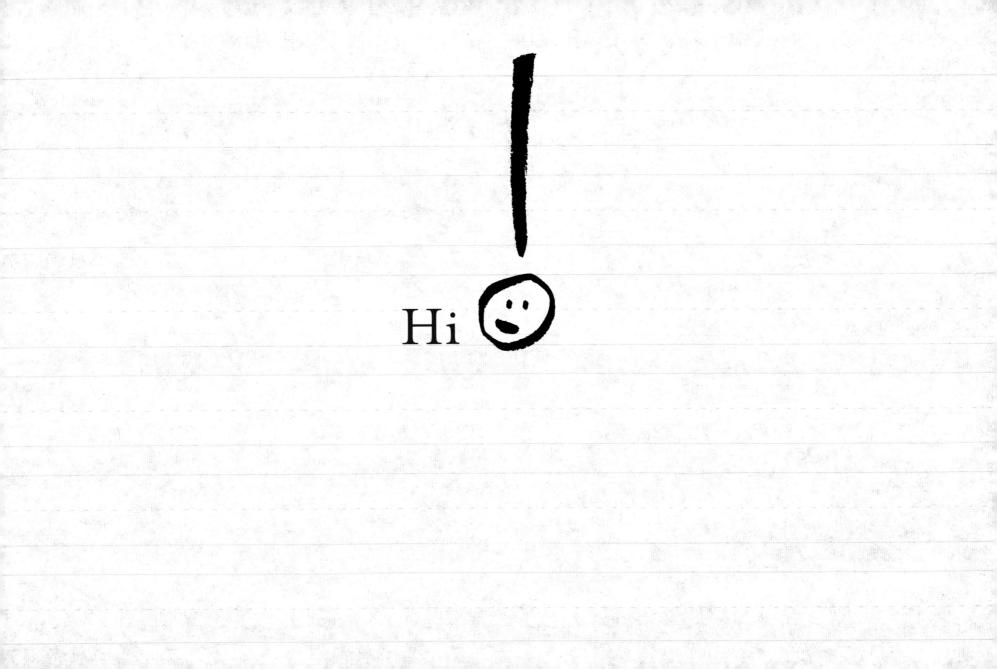

That felt right, so he tried something bigger.

Howdy!

And as he pushed himself a bit more,

he discovered a world of endless possibilities.

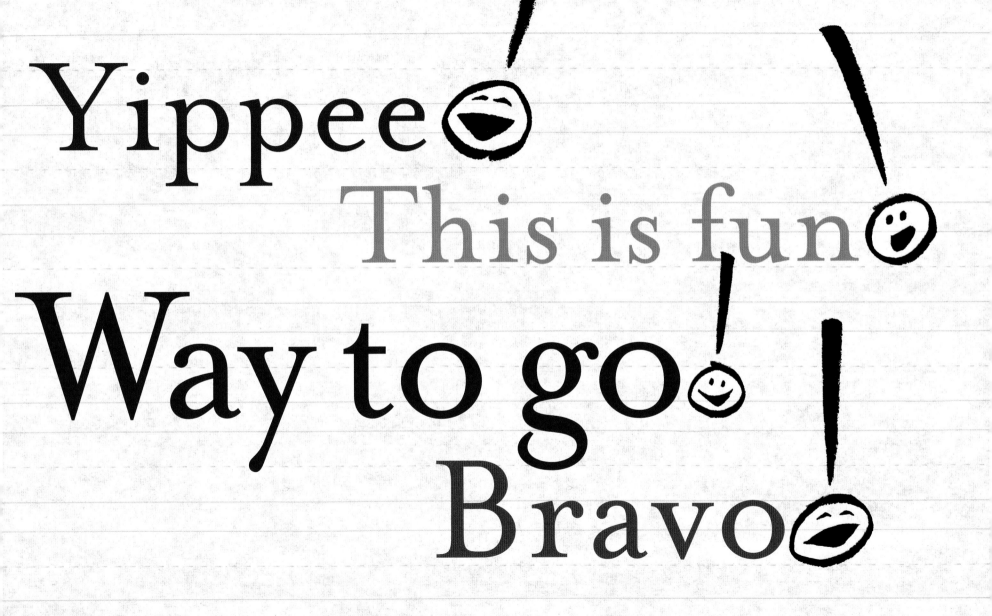

You're it!

It was like he broke free
from a life sentence.

Ye

Cool!

Yum!

That's great!

Thanks

S Home run

Congratulations

Happy Birthday

Go Encore

Look out

Wake up Boo

He couldn't wait to show everyone.

Hey guys, it's me

Of course, there was much exclaiming.

So, with his head held high,

he went off . . .

. . . to make his mark.

The end!

Text © 2013 Amy Krouse Rosenthal   •   Illustrations © 2013 Tom Lichtenheld

All rights reserved. Published by Scholastic Press, an imprint of Scholastic Inc.,

Publishers since 1920. SCHOLASTIC, SCHOLASTIC PRESS, and associated logos are

trademarks and/or registered trademarks of Scholastic Inc.

Library of Congress Control Number: 2012936803

Rosenthal, Amy Krouse. Exclamation Mark / [Text by] Amy Krouse Rosenthal ;

[Illustrations by] Tom Lichtenheld   p.   cm.

ISBN 978-0-545-43679-3

10 9 8 7 6 5 4   blastoff!   14 15 16 17

Printed in China   38

First edition, March 2013

Typeset in Brandon Grotesque and Mrs. Eaves.

The illustrations were rendered in ink and other exciting materials.

Book design by Tom Lichtenheld and Marijka Kostiw

We dedicate this book to Amy Rennert.

Thank you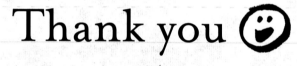

—Amy and Tom

*That reminds me,
did I ever thank you?*

*Hey, I ask the questions
around here, buddy!*